THE STUPIDS TAKE OFF

HARRY ALLARD · JAMES MARSHALL

Houghton Mifflin Company
Boston 1989

Also by Harry Allard and James Marshall

The Stupids Step Out
The Stupids Have a Ball
The Stupids Die

Miss Nelson Is Missing!
Miss Nelson Is Back
Miss Nelson Has a Field Day

Library of Congress Cataloging-in-Publication Data

Allard, Harry.
  The stupids take off / Harry Allard, James Marshall.
    p. cm.
  Summary: In an attempt to avoid a visit from Uncle Carbuncle, the
Stupids fly off in their airplane and visit several other relatives
who are just as stupid as they are.
  ISBN 0-395-50068-0
  [1. Humorous stories.] I. Marshall, James, 1942–   . II. Title.
PZ7.A413Su 1989   89-31719
[E] — dc19   CIP
              AC

Printed in the United States of America

H 10 9 8 7 6 5 4 3 2 1

For Alexandra Elise Daley

The Stupids were heavy sleepers.
It took a lot to get them going
in the morning.

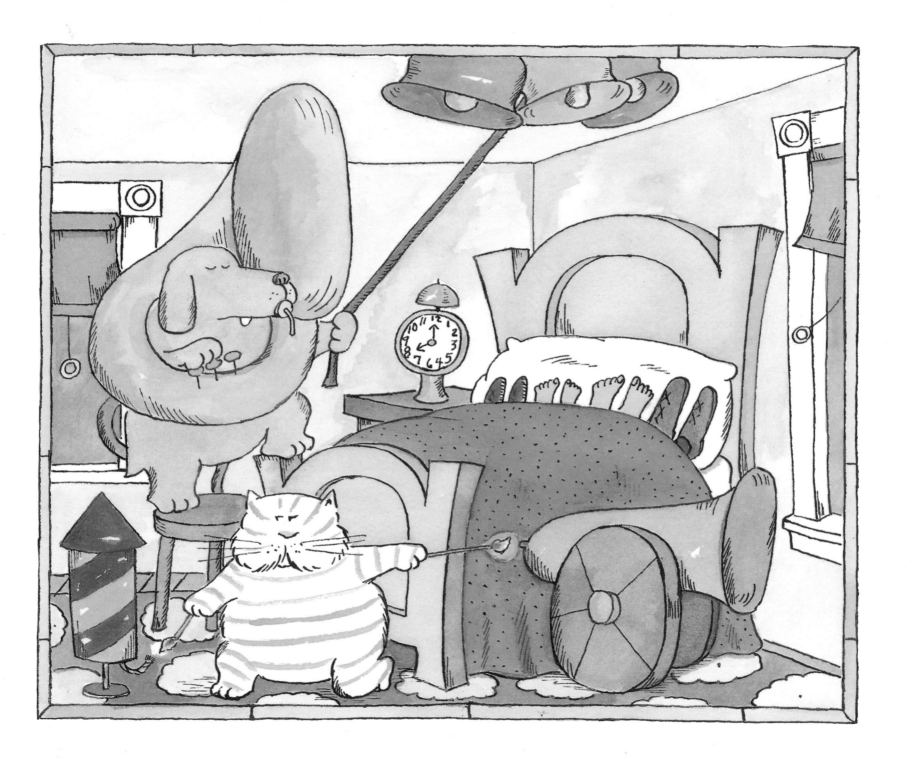

While Stanley Q. Stupid was brushing his teeth,
a telegram arrived.
"Egads!" cried Stanley.
"Uncle Carbuncle is coming!"
Mrs. Stupid let out a blood-curdling
scream from the kitchen.

The two Stupid kids had never heard of
Uncle Carbuncle.
While breakfast was hanging out to dry,
Mr. Stupid got out the family album.
"Uncle Carbuncle is pretty strong medicine,"
said Mrs. Stupid.
"Uncle Carbuncle is to be avoided at all costs,"
said Mr. Stupid. "Why don't we take our
vacation early this year?"
"Oh, we get it," said the two Stupid kids.

"Hurry up, hurry up!" cried Mr. Stupid.
"He could be here any moment!"
"I'm polishing my nails," said Mrs. Stupid.
"They've never looked prettier," said Mr. Stupid.
"Now let's get a move on!"

With their superb cat Xylophone at the controls,
and without a minute to spare, the Stupids took off.

At 10,000 feet the Stupids happened to pass
Cousin Fifi Stupid.
"Can't stop to talk," said Cousin Fifi.
"I'm off to Grandfather Stupid's graduation
from kindergarten. Au revoir!"
"Isn't Spanish a beautiful language?"
said Mrs. Stupid.

On the spur of the moment
the Stupids decided to attend
little Patty Stupid's sixth birthday party.
"Why are there eight candles
on the cake?" said Buster.
"Because I didn't have six," said Patty.
"That makes sense," said Buster.

Little Patty's father, Uncle Artichoke,
took the Stupids into the back yard
to show off his new diving board.
The Stupids were impressed.
"We really must get one of these,"
said Mr. Stupid.

Over in Spittoon Springs, the Stupids
ran into Farmer Joe Stupid,
who complained about this year's
poor crop of pencils.
"They just don't seem to want to grow,"
said Farmer Joe.
"Gosh," said Stanley.

As the Stupids flew away from Spittoon Springs,
Aunt Flossie Stupid waved from her front porch.
"That Aunt Flossie is a real doll," said Mrs. Stupid.

"Lunchtime!" called out Mrs. Stupid.
The Stupids stopped off at their favorite
seafood restaurant.
"Get your shoes off the table, kids,"
said Mrs. Stupid. "You don't want to soil them."
"Let's try the catch of the day,"
said Mr. Stupid.

Just to be nice, the Stupids made a quick visit
to Cousin Roscoe Stupid, who was
recovering from a bad case of the jitters.
The Stupids wore their silly masks
and made loud noises.
"Cousin Roscoe didn't seem happy
to see us," said Mr. Stupid.
"He's a little bizarre," said Mrs. Stupid.

When darkness fell, the Stupids headed for home.
"We managed to escape Uncle Carbuncle,"
said Petunia. "But we saw quite a few other relatives!"
"That's unavoidable," said Buster.
"The Stupids are everywhere."

Back home, the Stupids put on their
diving equipment and got ready for bed.
"Good night, dear," said Mrs. Stupid.
"We had quite a bit of fun today."
"Yes," said Mr. Stupid.
"That always happens sometimes."
And he pulled down the shade.